THE EAGLE HAS LANDED

Adapted by Lara Bergen
Based on the teleplay by Eric Weiner
Illustrated by Alisa Klayman-Grodsky

Based on the "Stanley" books created by
Griff with ticktock publishing, ltd.

Printed in the United States of America
First Edition
1 2 3 4 5 6 7 8 9 10
Library of Congress Catalog Card
Number: 2003096534
ISBN: 0-7868-4557-0

Stanley was playing eagle in the living room when all of a sudden he heard an important announcement on TV. In just one week, there would be a Kids' Kite Contest—with three BIG prizes to be given away!

"Whoa! I can win that contest!" Stanley cried. "I know I can!"

Right away, Stanley started to build a kite.
"What do you think?" he asked his dog, Harry;
his cat, Elsie; and his goldfish, Dennis.

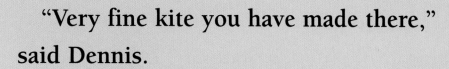

"Very fine kite you have made there," said Dennis.

"Kite?" said Harry as he jumped toward it. He thought the kite was a fetch toy.

"Just wait," Stanley told everybody. "This kite's going to fly higher than any kite any kid ever made! And next week . . . I'm going to win a prize!"

Then Stanley went outside to fly his kite. But it wasn't as easy as he had thought.

When he came back in, Dennis reminded him of one important thing. He still needed to *practice* flying his kite.

But Stanley had a very different idea....

Quickly, Stanley drew a picture and held it up. "I've got an awesome plan to make my kite fly," he said. "All I need is my new favorite animal in the whole wide world—the bald eagle."

According to Stanley's plan, he would hold one end of the kite string and the eagle would hold the other. Stanley could just imagine his kite soaring higher than any kite had ever done before. . . . But Dennis could see a few problems with Stanley's plan.

"Allow me to compliment you on a very creative solution," said Dennis. "But when you're learning to do something new, you really have to *practice*."

Then he looked at Stanley's drawing. "Bald eagles aren't really bald," he said. "They have snowy white feathers on their head, which make them look bald from a distance."

Stanley could see he had a bit more to learn about bald eagles. And what better place to learn than from *The Great Big Book of Everything*!

Stanley pulled out the book and turned the pages. "A . . . B . . . C . . . D . . . E—Eagles!"

"My, my!" Dennis exclaimed. "What big birds! When a bald eagle spreads its wings, they can stretch seven feet across." That would be as wide as Stanley's living room couch!

"They also have terrific eyesight," Dennis informed Stanley. "They can see at least four times farther away than a human can. That's why, when someone can see really well, we say they have an 'eagle eye.'"

But what Stanley really wanted to know was how eagles learn to fly. And the best way to learn about that, he decided, was to meet an eagle. So Stanley picked up Dennis's fishbowl . . . and the two jumped into *The Great Big Book of Everything*.

"Whoa! Where are we?" Stanley asked, looking all around him.

"I believe we're in an aerie," Dennis told him. "That's a nest in a high spot like an eagle's nest."

"It's huge!" Stanley exclaimed.

And so were the birds that lived in it!

But the aerie was home to more than just
an eagle mommy and daddy. It was also
home to some little eagle babies.

"It'll take almost three months before these babies are big enough to fly off on their own," Dennis told Stanley. "They need time to practice!"

"Practice . . . " Stanley repeated after Dennis. "Now why didn't you tell me that before?"

Dennis looked at Stanley and sighed.

At last, Stanley realized what he needed to do to get really good at kite flying.

"C'mon, Dennis!" Stanley shouted. "Let's go practice!" Stanley and Dennis waved good-bye to the eagles and jumped back into Stanley's room.

And Stanley did practice—every single day, until the contest. Then Stanley flew a new kite he had built. He named it "The Bald Eagle."

Everybody cheered! Stanley's kite flew higher than anybody else's. And the judges gave him a brand-new award—for the most birdlike kite they had ever seen!

That night, as Stanley lay in bed, he thought about how cool bald eagles really were.

"And just think," he said to Dennis, "they're not bald at all. Well, good night, Dennis."

Dennis smiled at his friend. "Good night, Champion Eagle-Flier Stanley," he whispered.

DID YOU KNOW?

- The bald eagle was chosen as the national bird of the United States of America in 1782.
- A bald eagle has approximately 7,000 feathers.
- A bald eagle's feathers weigh twice as much as its bones.
- Bald eagles like to eat fish. They snatch them out of the water with their sharp talons (or claws).

FILL IN THE PUZZLE WITH THE WORDS BELOW:

KITE

EAGLE

FEATHERS

WINGS

Special thanks to Steve Sarro, Curator of Birds at The Baltimore Zoo, for help with the "Did You Know?" facts